◫ READERS

Pre-level 1

Fishy Tales
Colorful Days
Garden Friends
Party Fun
In the Park
Farm Animals
Petting Zoo
Let's Make Music
Meet the Dinosaurs
Duck Pond Dip
My Dress-up Box

On the Move
Snakes Slither and Hiss
Family Vacation
Ponies and Horses
My Day
Monkeys
Big Trucks
John Deere: Busy Tractors
Lego Duplo: On the Farm
Cuentos de Peces en *español*
Dias Ilenos de color en *español*

Level 1

A Day at Greenhill Farm
Truck Trouble
Tale of a Tadpole
Surprise Puppy!
Duckling Days
A Day at Seagull Beach
Whatever the Weather
Busy Buzzy Bee
Big Machines
Wild Baby Animals
A Bed for the Winter
Born to be a Butterfly
Dinosaur's Day
Feeding Time
Diving Dolphin
Rockets and Spaceships
My Cat's Secret
First Day at Gymnastics
A Trip to the Zoo
I Can Swim!
A Trip to the Library
A Trip to the Doctor
A Trip to the Dentist
I Want to be a Ballerina
Animal Hide and Seek
Submarines and Submersibles
Animals at Home
Let's Play Soccer
Homes Around the World

Bugs and Us
Train Travel
LEGO: Trouble at the Bridge
LEGO: Secret at Dolphin Bay
Star Wars: What is a Wookie?
Star Wars: Ready, Set, Podrace!
Star Wars: Luke Skywalker's Amazing
    Story
Star Wars Clone Wars: Watch Out for
    Jabba the Hutt!
Star Wars Clone Wars: Pirates... and
    Worse
Power Rangers: Jungle Fury: We are the
    Power Rangers
Lego Duplo: Around Town
Indiana Jones: Indy's Adventures
John Deere: Good Morning, Farm!
A Day in the Life of a Builder
A Day in the Life of a Dancer
A Day in the Life of a Firefighter
A Day in the Life of a Teacher
A Day in the Life of a Musician
A Day in the Life of a Doctor
A Day in the Life of a Police Officer
A Day in the Life of a TV Reporter
Gigantes de Hierro en *español*
Crías del mundo animal en *español*

A Note to Parents

DK READERS is a compelling program for beginning readers, designed in conjunction with leading literacy experts, including Dr. Linda Gambrell, Distinguished Professor of Education at Clemson University. Dr. Gambrell has served as President of the National Reading Conference, the College Reading Association, and the International Reading Association.

Beautiful illustrations and superb full-color photographs combine with engaging, easy-to-read stories to offer a fresh approach to each subject in the series. Each DK READER is guaranteed to capture a child's interest while developing his or her reading skills, general knowledge, and love of reading.

The five levels of DK READERS are aimed at different reading abilities, enabling you to choose the books that are exactly right for your child:

Pre-level 1: Learning to read
Level 1: Beginning to read
Level 2: Beginning to read alone
Level 3: Reading alone
Level 4: Proficient readers

The "normal" age at which a child begins to read can be anywhere from three to eight years old. Adult participation through the lower levels is very helpful for providing encouragement, discussing storylines, and sounding out unfamiliar words.

No matter which level you select, you can be sure that you are helping your child learn to read, then read to learn!

LONDON, NEW YORK, MUNICH,
MELBOURNE, AND DELHI

Series Editor Deborah Lock, Penny Smith
Art Editor Jacqueline Gooden
U.S. Editors Elizabeth Hester, John Searcy
Pre-production Francesca Wardell
Jacket Designer Natalie Godwin

Reading Consultant
Linda Gambrell, Ph.D.

First American Edition, 2005
This edition, 2013
Published in the United States by DK Publishing, Inc.
375 Hudson Street, New York, New York 10014

13 14 15 16 17 10 9 8 7 6 5 4 3 2 1
002—192121—July/2013

Copyright © 2005, 2013 Dorling Kindersley Limited

Published in Great Britain by Dorling Kindersley Limited.

A catalog record for this book is available
from the Library of Congress

ISBN: 978-1-4654-0944-7 (Paperback)
ISBN: 978-1-4654-0945-4 (Hardcover)

Color reproduction by Colourscan, Singapore
Printed and bound in China by L Rex Printing Co., Ltd.

The publisher would like to thank the following for their kind
permission to reproduce their photographs:
a=above; c=center; b=below; l=left; r=right; t=top

Alamy Images: Comstock Images 22-23; Bruce Coleman Inc 27t;
BSH Stock 14t; Colin Harris/ LightTouch Images 8bl; FLPA 16bl;
gopi 9bcr; Greg Philpott 9bc; Ian Miles/ Flashpoint Pictures 9bl; Ivor
Toms 9br; Lynne Siler/ Focus Group 8br; Mark Sykes 8bcr, 32tc;
Robography 9bcl; Stock Connection Distribution 15b. **Corbis:** Ariel
Skelley 11, 20b; Geoff Moon; Frank Lane Picture Agency 17bcl, 17t;
Kevin Fleming 6t; Kevin Schafer 17bl, 17br, 32cra; Najlah Feanny
28-29; Norbert Schaefer 26c; Scott T. Smith 17bcr; Tom Stewart
30-31. **DK Images:** Philip Dowell 29bc. **Getty Images:** Andy Sacks
12-13; Peter Cade 24-25; Robert Daly 18-19; Yellow Dog
Productions 8-9. **N.H.P.A.:** Ernie Janes 16br. **Zefa Visual Media:**
Masterfile / Kevin Dodge 4-5; Noel Hendrickson 16t.

All other images © Dorling Kindersley
For more information see: www.dkimages.com

Discover more at
www.dk.com

 **READERS**

Petting Zoo

DK Publishing

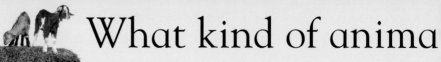 What kind of anima

We are at the
petting zoo.

o you see here?

We are petting
a drowsy donkey.

 donkeys

ear

hoof

We are walking two baby llamas.

llamas

leash

I am brushing a pony's coat.

mane

 ponies

 pigs

I am picking up
a little pink pig.

snout

hoof

hen

chicks

I am carrying
a soft yellow chick.

chick

 stick insects

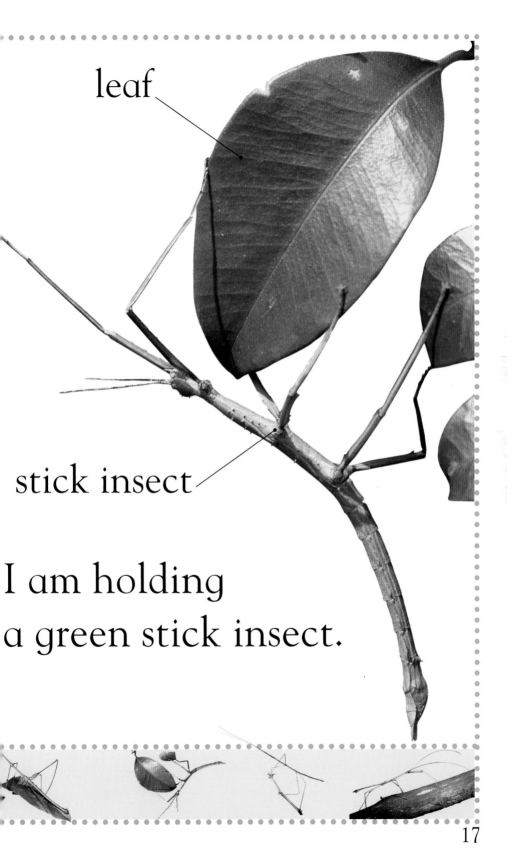

leaf

stick insect

I am holding
a green stick insect.

 frogs

I am watching
a beady-eyed frog.

Ribbit! Ribbit!

toe

It is mealtime now.
I give the woolly lamb
some milk.

 lambs

wool

I am feeding
a hungry rabbit.

ear

carrot

rabbits

This fluffy guinea pig
is nibbling a leaf.

 guinea pigs

whiskers

claws

The white goose
wants a snack.

 geese

gosling

bill

feathers

 goats

This long-horned goat is eating his lunch.

horn

Goodbye, animals!